가성비갑
영어회화 대화
대박 많은 책

가성비갑 영어회화 대화 대박 많은 책

발   행 | 2019년 4월 25일

저   자 | 김지완

펴낸이 | 한건희

펴낸곳 | 주식회사 부크크

출판사등록 | 2014.07.15.(제2014-16호)

주   소 | 경기도 부천시 원미구 춘의동 202 춘의테크노파크 2단지 202동 1306호

전   화 | 1670-8316

이메일 | info@bookk.co.kr

ISBN | 979-11-272-7038-4

www.bookk.co.kr

가성비갑
영어회화 대화
대박 많은 책

김지완 지음

CONTENTS

대박 대화 01 10
대박 대화 02 11
대박 대화 03 12
대박 대화 04 13
대박 대화 05 14
대박 대화 06 15
대박 대화 07 16
대박 대화 08 17
대박 대화 09 18
대박 대화 10 19
대박 대화 11 20
대박 대화 12 21
대박 대화 13 22
대박 대화 14 23
대박 대화 15 24
대박 대화 16 25
대박 대화 17 26
대박 대화 18 27
대박 대화 19 28
대박 대화 20 29
대박 대화 21 30
대박 대화 22 31
대박 대화 23 32
대박 대화 24 33
대박 대화 25 34

대박 대화 26 35
대박 대화 27 36
대박 대화 28 37
대박 대화 29 38
대박 대화 30 39
대박 대화 31 40
대박 대화 32 41
대박 대화 33 42
대박 대화 34 43
대박 대화 35 44
대박 대화 36 45
대박 대화 37 46
대박 대화 38 47
대박 대화 39 48
대박 대화 40 49
대박 대화 41 50
대박 대화 42 51
대박 대화 43 52
대박 대화 44 53
대박 대화 45 54
대박 대화 46 55
대박 대화 47 56
대박 대화 48 57
대박 대화 49 58
대박 대화 50 59

대박 대화 51 60
대박 대화 52 61
대박 대화 53 62
대박 대화 54 63
대박 대화 55 64
대박 대화 56 65

대박 대화 57 66
대박 대화 58 67
대박 대화 59 68
대박 대화 60 69
랜덤 테스트 71

영어회화 대화
대박 많은 책, 가성비 갑!

영어회화 대화 대박 많은 영어책,
다른 회화책 더 이상 필요 없다!

국내 최고 많은 영어회화 대화를
수록했습니다. 영어회화, 작문 어떤 것을
하든 문제 없는 대화 표현 수록.
더 이상 어설프게 영어회화를 다룬 책은
필요 없습니다.

영어회화 필수만!

스피킹이면 스피킹, 라이팅이면 라이팅
다 문제 없다!

영어회화가 말하기에만 쓰고 라이팅에만
쓸 리가 있나요?
문어체, 구어체 구별이 필요 없는 시대
대화만 익히면 영어 문장 만들기는
문제 없어요.

영어회화 대화 대박 모음

A: I haven't eaten anything since 10 a.m.
B: Me neither. Some snack this morning is all I've eaten today.
A: 전 아침 10시 이후로 아무것도 못 먹었어요.
B: 저도요. 오늘 아침에 간식 먹은 게 다예요.

A: What's the biggest sport in Korea apart from football?
B: Well, lots of people are into baseball and basketball is really popular, too.
A: 축구를 제외하고 한국에서 가장 큰 스포츠가 뭐에요?
B: 음, 많은 사람들이 야구에 빠져 있고 농구도 매우 인기 있어요.

A: What is this? This smells fishy.
B: Of course, because it's tuna kimchi soup.
A: I don't like it.
A: 이게 뭐야? 비린내가 나.
B: 당연하지. 참치 김치찌개니까 그렇지.
A: 난 그걸 좋아하지 않아.

대화 02

B: I haven't even asked her to go out.
A: Why not?
B: I don't know, but I can't stop thinking about her. She's super smart and pretty attractive.
B: 아직 그녀한테 데이트 신청도 안 했어.
A: 왜 안했어?
B: 나도 모르겠어. 하지만 그녀 생각을 멈출 수가 없어. 그녀는 무지하게 똑똑하고 매력적이야.

A: You need to talk to Jinsu.
B: He's never gonna answer his cell.
A: We're gonna see him later.
B. I'll talk to him tonight.
A: 넌 진수와 얘기 좀 해야 해.
B: 걘 절대로 전화를 받으려 하지 않을 거야.
A: 우린 나중에 그를 만나게 될 거야.
B: 오늘 저녁에 걔한테 말해볼게.

대화 03

A: We've got a lot to do.
B: This overtime is making me crazy.
A: 우린 아직 할 일이 많아요.
B: 이 초과근무 때문에 짜증나요.

A: That snow just isn't going to stop!
B: I know. It took me an hour just to shovel the driveway before I left today.
A: 눈이 그칠 것 같지 않네요!
B: 그러니까요. 오늘 출발하기 전에 진입로까지 삽질을 하느라 한 시간이나 걸렸어요.

A: I could eat ramyon every meal of the day.
B: That doesn't sound very healthy.
A: 나는 끼니마다 다 라면을 먹을 수도 있어.
B: 그건 그렇게 건강에 좋을 것 같지 않아.

대화 04

A: I decided to spend all day at the public library.
B: Sounds really motivating.
A: 나는 공공 도서관에서 하루 종일 시간을 보내기로 했어.
B: 정말 의욕적인 것 같네.

A: We really need to get out more.
B: So, will you come to the movies with me?
A: 우린 좀 더 자주 나가서 놀아야 할 것 같아.
B: 그럼, 나랑 영화 보러 갈래?

A: I'm really in the mood for a drink.
B: Yes, let's stop off at the bar across the bank.
A: 진짜 한잔 하고 싶은데.
B: 그래. 은행 길건너에 있는 바에 들르자.

대화 05

A: I'm planning on taking the family to England. Have you ever been there?
B: Yes, in fact I went last summer.
A: 영국으로 가족을 데리고 가려고요. 가본 적 있어요?
B: 네, 사실 지난 여름에 갔었어요.

A: What about the dinner? Did you enjoy the food?
B: I love Korean cuisine. Thanks for your treat.
A: 저녁 식사는 어떠셨나요? 음식이 괜찮았나요?
B: 전 한국 음식을 좋아해요. 대접해 주셔서 고마워요.

A: I love it when the week winds down.
B: Yes, we can spend more time with our family.
A: 나는 한 주가 끝나가는 주말이 참 좋아.
B: 그래, 우리 가족들이랑 시간을 더 많이 보낼 수가 있잖아.

대화 06

A: Are you in a hurry?
B: Yes, my friend is waiting for me in the car.
A: 바쁘세요?
B: 네, 친구가 차에서 기다리고 있어요.

A: My son slept late this morning, so I have to drop off him at school.
B: Oh, it's already 8 o'clock. Hurry up, but drive safely.
A: 아들이 아침에 늦잠을 자서 아들을 학교에 내려 줘야 해요.
B: 어머, 벌써 8시에요. 서둘러요, 하지만 조심히 운전하고요.

A: Do you have any aspirin?
B: Yeah, why?
A: I have a fever.
A: 아스피린 있니?
B: 응, 왜?
A: 열이 있어서.

대화 07

A: Look at this picture. I want to take those trains sometime.
B: Then why don't we try sometime this month?
A: Sounds nice. Let's decide when to go.
A: 이 사진 좀 봐. 언젠가는 그 기차들을 타보고 싶어.
B: 그럼 우리 이번 달에 한번 타보는 게 어때?
A: 좋아. 우리 언제 갈지 결정하자.

A: I think we can use this display picture in our advertisement.
B: That's a great idea. How about this one?
A: 이 상품 사진을 저희 광고에도 사용할 수 있을 것 같은데요.
B: 좋은 생각이에요. 이건 어때요?

A: How far are you going to hike today?
B: I'm going to make it to the hospital. That's about six miles.
A: 오늘 얼마나 하이킹할 거야?
B: 병원까지 가야지. 6마일이쯤 돼.

대화 08

A: Where are you going?
B: I'm gonna go to the movies.
A: You better get going. There's gonna be a long line.
A: 뭐 할 거니?
B: 영화 보러 가게 될 거야.
A: 지금 가는 게 좋을 거야. 줄이 길 거거든.

A: Do you have time to go to the symphony with me?
B: When would you like to go?
A: 저랑 음악회에 갈 시간 있으세요?
B: 언제 가고 싶으신데요?

A: What is that? It tastes like chicken.
A: We should get the recipe.
A: 그거 뭐야? 닭고기 맛이 나.
B: 만드는 법을 알아가야 겠다.

대화 09

A: You're taller than average. How tall are you?
B: One meter 87 centimeters.
A: 당신은 보통 사람보다 키가 좀 크군요. 키가 얼마나 되요?
B: 1미터 87센티미터에요.

A: I'd like to take a shuttle bus. Where can I buy a ticket?
B: You may stand in line here.
A: 셔틀버스를 타려고 하는데요. 티켓은 어디서 사나요?
B: 여기 줄을 서면 됩니다.

A: I sleep through the alarm very often.
B: Set your smartphone alarm for three times.
A: 난 자주 알람소리를 못 듣고 자.
B: 스마트폰 알람을 세 번 맞춰 놓아봐.

대화 10

A: How do you like the atmosphere at this place?
B: It's actually hopping.
B: Then, we can stay a little longer.
A: 여기 분위기 어때?
B: 팔팔한데.
B: 그러면 좀 더 있자.

A: How long does it take to get to Wall Street?
B: It depends on the traffic.
A: 월스트리트까지 얼마나 걸리나요?
B: 교통 상황에 달려 있어요.

A: I'll see you tomorrow at the zoo! I hope it doesn't rain.
B: I'm sure the weather will be fine. Make sure you bring your lunch.
A: 내일 동물원에서 보자! 비가 안 왔으면 좋겠다.
B: 날씨는 좋을 거야. 점심 싸오는 거 잊지 마.

대화 11

A: What kind of car would you like to rent?
B: A small car with good gas mileage, if possible.
A: 어떤 종류를 렌트하려고 하시죠?
B: 되도록 연비가 좋은 소형차요.

A: We're going to eat dinner together tonight.
B: Since I don't drink, I'll be the designated driver.
A: 오늘 다 같이 저녁 회식을 할 거에요.
B: 전 술을 마시지 않으니까, 제가 운전해 드릴게요.

A: I hope we aren't late.
B: I don't think we'll be late. I'll drive a little faster.
A: 우리 늦지 않았으면 좋겠다.
B: 늦지 않을 거야. 좀 더 빨리 운전할게.

대화 12

A: Did you quit drinking?
B: Yes, I quit by myself for my health.
A: 술 끊었어?
B: 응, 건강을 생각해서 스스로 끊었어.

A: We shouldn't be in here. We're gonna get in trouble.
B: You should just leave if you're that worried.
A: 우린 여기 있으면 안 돼. 곤란을 겪게 될 거야.
B: 그렇게 걱정이 되면 넌 그냥 가는 게 좋겠다.

A: I'd really appreciate if you could watch the kids tonight.
B: Do you have to work late?
A: 오늘 밤 애들을 봐준다면 정말 고맙겠어.
B: 야근해야 해?

대화 13

A: Are you ready to order drinks?
B: Yes. I'll have a glass of wine.
A: What kind of wine do you prefer?
B: It doesn't matter to me.
A: 주문하시겠어요?
B: 네, 와인으로 하죠.
A: 어떤 와인이 좋으세요?
B: 아무거나 상관없어요.

A: Have you found a job yet?
B: No. I swear I'm gonna get a job.
A: It's gonna be okay.
A: 아직 취직 안 했어?
B: 안 했어. 맹세코 꼭 취직을 할 거야.
A: 그건 잘 될 거야.

A: How the hell did you get hurt?
B: I just fell down.
A: 도대체 너 어떻게 다치게 된 거야?
B: 그냥 넘어졌어.

대화 14

A: What's taking so long?
B: I can't get this machine to start.
A: The supervisor's going to get mad.
B: I'm working on it!
A: 왜 그렇게 오래 걸렸어?
B: 이 기계를 작동시킬 수가 없어.
A: 상사가 화를 낼 거야.
B: 지금 노력 중이야!

A: How long will it take to fix it?
B: It's gonna be a few minutes.
A: OK. I can wait. It's gonna be fine.
A: I hope you're right.
A: 고치는 데 얼마나 걸려?
B: 몇 분 걸리게 될 거야.
A: 알았어. 기다릴게. 잘 될 거야.
B: 그랬으면 좋겠다.

대화 15

A: We will have to get there early to get a seat.
B: I normally get there early. I'll save you a seat.
A: 자리를 맡으려면 우리 일찍 가야 할 것 같아.
B: 난 보통 일찍 가니까. 내가 네 자리도 맡아 놓을게.

A: These are the best pizza I've ever eaten.
B: Yeah, I have to ask the cook for the recipe.
A: 이건 정말 여태까지 먹어본 중에 최고의 피자네요.
B: 네, 주방장에게 만드는 법을 물어봐야겠어요.

A: What should we do with these leftovers?
B: Let's eat them tomorrow morning.
A: 이 남은 음식들은 어떻게 하지?
B: 내일 아침에 먹자.

대화 16

A: Have you ever been on a blind date?
B: Yes, just once in the past.
A: When was the last time you dated her?
B: About two years ago.
A: 너 소개팅 해본 적 있어?
B: 응, 전에 딱 한 번 해봤어.
A: 그 여자랑 마지막으로 데이트한 게 언제였어?
B: 2년 전쯤 됐어.

A: Don't you miss the comforts of home?
B: Sure. I miss home-cooked meals sometimes.
A: 집에 있을 때의 편안함이 그립지 않으세요?
B: 그렇죠. 가끔은 집에서 만든 음식이 그립죠.

A: You and Steve seem pretty tight. How long have you known each other?
B: We go way back. I've known him since kindergarten.
A: 너하고 스티브 꽤 친한 것 같은데. 알고 지낸지 얼마나 됐어?
B: 안 지 한참 됐어. 유치원 때부터 알고 지냈지.

대화 17

A: I think you drank too much.
B: I'm getting dizzy.
A: You shouldn't drive.
B: You're right. So, will you drive me home?
A: 너 과음한 것 같아.
B: 어지러워지기 시작하고 있어.
A: 운전하면 안 돼.
B: 맞아. 그럼 네가 날 집에 태워다줄래?

A: How often do you drink?
B: Just about everyday.
A: You're kidding. I think you should cut down.
A: 술은 얼마나 자주 드세요?
B: 거의 매일 마시죠.
A: 정말이에요? 술을 줄이셔야겠어요.

대화 18

A: My friend and I got in a big fight.
B: So, how're you gonna make this right?
A: I'm gonna apologize her.
B. That's a good start.
A: 내 친구하고 크게 다퉜어.
B: 그래서 어떻게 해결할 건데?
A: 가서 그녀에게 사과하려고.
B: 좋은 시작이야.

A: What kind of movies do you like?
B: I like to watch animated movies.
A: 어떤 장르의 영화를 좋아해요?
B: 만화영화를 좋아해요.

A: Do yoy take care of your pet?
B: No, my brother always feeds him every day.
A: That's nice.
A: 네가 애완동물을 돌보니?
B: 아니, 우리 형이 매일 먹이를 줘.
A: 와 정말 착한걸.

대화 19

A: I always have trouble following directions.
B: You overcooked your meal.
A: 요리법을 따라 하는 게 항상 어려워.
B: 너 또 음식 태웠구나.

A: How did you like the movie?
B: It was pretty boring.
A: Oh, really? I thought it was great.
B: Really? I didn't know you like this kind of films.
A: 영화 어땠어?
B: 정말 지루했어.
A: 오, 그래? 난 정말 좋았는데.
B: 정말? 네가 그런 영화를 좋아하는 줄 몰랐어.

A: Do you think she likes me?
B: I'm sure she likes you.
A: 그녀가 나를 좋아할까?
B: 그녀가 분명히 널 좋아할 거야.

대화 20

A: Ally is having a hard time with her projects.

B: Wasn't she promoted recently?

A: Yes. So she has a lot of works to do now.

A: 알리가 일 때문에 힘들어해요.

B: 얼마 전에 승진하지 않았어요?

A: 맞아요. 그래서 지금 할 일이 많아요.

B: Are you still paying the loan?

A: Yes. I have to pay them for ten years, and this is her seventh year.

B: Oh, since interests have gone up, I guess you have to pay more.

B: 당신 아직도 대출 갚고 있어요?

A: 네, 10년 동안 갚아야 하는데, 올해가 7년째에요.

B: 이자가 높아져서 더 많이 갚아야겠네요.

A: I think it's time for the presentation.

B: Are you nervous?

A: Yes, I'm so nervous.

A: 발표를 할 때가 된 것 같아.

B: 긴장되니?

A: 응, 너무 긴장이 돼.

대화 21

A: I didn't know you here. I wanna grab a drink.
B: Mind if I join you?
A: That sounds great.
A: 여기 있는 줄 몰랐네. 한 잔 하고 싶은데.
B: 내가 같이 가도 괜찮아?
A: 그러면 좋지.

A: What do you like most about traveling?
B: I love to discover new things.
A: 여행하면서 제일 좋은 게 뭔가요?
B: 새로운 것들을 발견하는 게 너무 좋아요.

A: I thought you were gone for good.
B. I only went to the store.
A: 네가 아주 가버린 줄 알았어.
B: 가게에 갔었던 거야.

대화 22

A: Wow, this movie was amazing! It kept me on the edge of my seat the whole time.
B: The special effects were fascinating, but the storyline was too predictable.
A: 와, 이 영화 대단했어! 끝까지 손에 땀을 쥐고 봤는데.
B: 특수 효과는 대단했지만 줄거리가 너무 뻔하잖아.

A: I need something to wake me up.
B: Coffee is kind of a pick-me-up.
A: Sounds good to me. A cup of coffee contain high levels of caffeine.
A: 나 잠을 깰 수 있는 뭔가가 필요해.
B: 커피가 나한테는 기운 나게 해주는 거야.
A: 그거 좋다. 커피 한 잔에는 카페인이 많이 들었어.

A: I didn't have any dinner.
B: That doesn't mean you can eat chips and cookies.
A: 저녁을 전혀 안 먹었어.
B: 그래서 과자를 먹어도 되는 건 아니야.

대화 23

A: Who's starring in the movie?
B: Tom Cruise is playing the lead.
A: Really? He's my favorite actor.
B: And Cameron Diaz is playing opposite of him, and a slew of top actors will play the supporting characters.
A: 그 영화의 주연이 누군데?
B: 톰 크루즈가 주연이야.
A: 그래? 내가 제일 좋아하는 배우야.
B: 카메론 디아즈가 상대역으로 나와.

A: Are you heading down to the mall tonight?
B: Yes, I'm going to go to the M-mall right now.
A: 오늘 밤 쇼핑몰에 갈 거니?
B: 응, 나 지금 M몰에 갈 거야.

A: How would you like your eggs?
B: Over easy, please. I'll make the toast.
A: 달걀 어떻게 해줄까?
B: 양쪽 다 익혀 줘. 난 토스트 만들게.

대화 24

A: I just got back from vacation.
A: How was it?
B: It was amazing!
A: I might start planning a trip.
A: 나 방금 휴가에서 돌아왔어.
A: 어땠어?
B: 환상적이었어!
A: 여행 계획부터 세워야겠다.

A: Do I have to keep going straight?
B: You should turn right at the next intersection.
A: 계속 죽 가야 하나요?
B: 다음 교차로에서 우회전해야 합니다.

A: How many times do you go to the ski report each year?
B: I try to make it to at least three or four.
A: 일 년에 스키장에는 몇 번이나 가니?
B: 난 적어도 서너 번은 가려고 하지.

대화 25

A: I'm sorry, we're fully booked tomorrow evening.
B: Could you put me on the waiting list in case of cancellations?
A: 죄송합니다. 내일 저녁에는 예약이 꽉 찼습니다.
B: 누가 취소할지 모르니 대기자 명단에 올려주실래요?

A: How do you want your reservation changed?
B: I'd like to change it from next Monday to Tuesday.
A: 예약을 어떻게 변경하시겠습니까?
B: 다음 주 월요일에서 화요일로 바꾸고 싶습니다.

A: Do you know this band? I first encounter this band on the radio.
A: I know them. I hear they are big in Europe.
A: 이 밴드 알아? 난 이 밴드를 라디오에서 처음 접했어.
B: 나도 알아. 그들은 유럽에서 굉장히 유명하대.

대화 26

A: When is the report due?
B: Tomorrow morning.
A: Can you handle it by yourself?
B: Of course, I can. I wanna finish this tonight.
A: 언제 보고서 마감일이지?
B: 내일 아침이야.
A: 혼자서 끝낼 수 있어?
B: 물론이지. 오늘 밤에 끝내고 싶어.

A: Oh, I'm dying for some chocolate or coffee.
B: Do you want some chocolate?
A: 아, 초콜릿이나 커피가 너무 먹고 싶어.
B: 초콜릿 좀 먹을래?

A: Do you ever play any sports?
B: Sure, I play basketball with my friends every Saturday.
A: 너는 운동 같은 거 하니?
B: 그럼, 친구들과 매주 토요일마다 농구해.

대화 27

A: My foods are overcooked and her potatoes are raw.
B: I apologize for them. I'll replace them straight away.
A: 제 음식이 너무 푹 익었고요. 감자는 덜 익었어요.
B: 음식이 그렇게 되다니 죄송합니다. 바로 바꿔드릴게요.

A: I'm gonna go get a drink. Do you want one?
B: Sure. What do you wanna do about it?
A: I wanna talk with you.
A: 술 마시러 갈 건데. 한 잔 할래?
B: 그러지. 그래서 어떻게 하고 싶은데?
A: 너랑 얘기 좀 하고 싶어.

A: Do you have a thermometer?
B: No, I used to have one, but it broke.
A: 우리 온도계 있어?
B: 아니, 전에 하나 있었는데, 고장 났어.

대화 28

A: What are you doing here?
B: I just wanted to talk.
A: Are we gonna talk about what happened today?
B: I'd like to talk about that.
A: 여기서 뭐하고 있어?
B: 그냥 얘기 좀 하고 싶었을 뿐이야.
A: 자, 이제 우리, 오늘 일어난 일에 대해 얘기해볼까?
B: 그 얘기 좀 했으면 해.

A: Why are you wearing a backpack?
B: A backpack is convenient when you're walking.
A: 왜 배낭을 메고 계세요?
B: 배낭이 걸을 때 편리하거든요.

A: How long has it been since you've had cancer?
B: I was diagnosed 5 years ago. I still have cancer.
A: 암에 걸린 지 얼마나 됐니?
B: 5년 전에 진단 받았어. 아직도 암 투병 중이야.

대화 29

A: Do you want some help?
B: That would be great!
A: I'm gonna go get some coffee.
A: 도움이 필요해?
B: 그러면 좋지!
A: 가서 커피를 가지고 올게.

A: Oh, I'm sorry to interrupt you. I saw you talking on the phone, so...
B: No, it's okay. Come on in and have a seat. Let's talk.
A: 아, 방해해서 죄송해요. 전화 통화 중이신거 같았는데..
B: 아니에요, 괜찮아요. 들어와서 앉으세요. 우리 얘기해요.

A: Do you get along with your friends?
B: Of course, we do. We're really tight.
A: I'm jealous.
A: 넌 친구들과 사이 좋아?
B: 그럼. 아주 친해.
A: 부럽다.

대화 30

A: I don't want to talk to you ever again.
B: I just wanted to apologize.
A: Please leave.
A: 너랑 다시는 말하고 싶지 않아.
B: 그냥 사과를 하고 싶었을 뿐이야.
A: 그냥 가줘.

A: Oh, I'm sorry to interrupt you.
B: It's okay.
A: Oh, your phone is ringing again.
B: I can get it later.
A: 아, 방해해서 죄송해요.
B: 괜찮아요.
A: 아, 전화가 또 왔네요.
B: 나중에 받으면 돼요.

A: It's so windy! I don't think I can stand up.
B. It looks like it's going to storm.
A: 바람이 엄청 많이 부네! 서 있을 수 없을 것 같아.
B: 폭풍우 올 것 같아.

대화 31

A: I want to tell you how sorry I am.
B: I don't feel well.
A: Please give me another chance.
A: 내가 얼마나 미안해 하고 있는지 말해주고 싶어.
B: 기분이 별로야.
A: 기회를 한 번만 더 줘.

A: Do you see anything you like?
B: Yes, that dress looks really nice.
A: Would you like to try it on?
A: 맘에 드는 것 고르셨어요?
B: 네, 저 드레스가 정말 멋진 것 같아요.
A: 한번 입어 보시겠어요?

A: How long have you had your pet?
B: We got him when he was only a puppy.
A: 얼마나 오랫동안 애완동물을 키웠니?
B: 강아지가 새끼였을 때 우리가 데려왔어.

대화 32

A: Hi. May I take your order?
B: Can I have a small, iced caramel macchiato with an extra shot?
A: 안녕하세요. 주문하실래요?
B: 아이스 캐러멜 마키아토 스몰 사이즈에 샷을 추가해주시겠어요?

A: Where is a good place to eat around here?
B: Any place in the square is good.
A: Thank you for the information.
A: 주위에 식사할 만한 괜찮은 곳 있나요?
B: 광장에 있는 식당은 다 괜찮아요.
A: 알려주셔서 감사합니다.

A: You look familiar. Do you happen to know my sister?
B: Yes! I know who you are. Aren't you Mira?
A: 당신은 낯이 익은데요. 혹시 저 알아요?
B: 네! 당신이 누군지 알아요. 미라 아니에요?

대화 33

A: What's on your shopping list for today?
B: I have to buy some apples and milk.
A: I need to get some butter.
B: Okay, let's get going then.
A: 오늘 쇼핑할 품목은 뭐지?
B: 사과랑 우유를 사야 돼.
A: 난 버터가 필요해.
B: 좋아, 그럼 가자.

A: Do you have any role models?
B: Yes, I do. My role model is Steve Jobs.
A: 너는 닮고 싶은 사람이 있니?
B: 응, 있어. 내 롤모델은 스티브 잡스야.

A: How did it go?
B: It went pretty well.
A: Can you please fill me in on the details?
A: 회의는 어땠나요?
B: 아주 잘 진행되었어요.
A: 자세한 내용을 좀 알려주시겠어요?

대화 34

A: Where is the grocery store?
B: Take the escalator to the second floor and it will be on the right.
A: 식료품점이 어디예요?
B: 에스컬레이터를 타고 2층으로 올라가면 오른쪽에 있습니다.

A: What can I do for you?
B: Where is perfume? I want one as a gift for my wife.
A: 무엇을 도와드릴까요?
B: 향수 어디 있나요? 아내한테 줄 선물로 하나 사고 싶어요.

A: I just don't know how we'll get this done.
B: Let's get some beer before we get started.
A: 난 어떻게 우리가 이걸 해낼지 정말 모르겠어.
B: 시작하기 전에 맥주 좀 마시고 하자.

대화 35

A: Do you have plans for today?
B: No. Holidays are just not my thing.
A: Are you serious? I love holidays.
B: I'd rather be sleeping.
A: 오늘 뭐 할 일 있어?
B: 아니. 나는 휴일이 별로야.
A: 정말이야? 난 휴일이 좋아.
B: 나는 그냥 잠이나 잘래.

A: Can I exchange these pants for a smaller size?
B: Do you have a receipt?
A: 이 바지를 작은 사이즈로 바꿔주시겠어요?
B: 영수증 있으세요?

A: Do you happen to know how to make kimchi stew?
B: I can give you a really great recipe .
A: 혹시 김치째개 만드는 방법을 알고 있니?
B: 내가 정말 훌륭한 요리법을 알려줄 수 있어.

대화 36

A: Did you get that on sale?
B: I sure did. There's a big sale at the department store.
A: Is the sale still going on?
A: 너 저거 세일 때 샀어?
B: 물론 그랬지. 백화점에서 바겐세일을 했었거든.
A: 아직도 세일하고 있을까?

A: I'm so happy for you.
B: Yeah, I finally got a promotion.
A: Yes, you have been working so hard lately.
A: 당신 참 잘됐어요.
B: 드디어 승진을 했죠.
A: 네, 당신 요즘 정말 일을 열심히 했잖아요.

A: How would you like your eggs? Sunnyside up, over medium?
B: Just over-easy for me.
A: 당신 달걀 어떻게 해줄까? 한쪽만 익혀 줄까, 아니면 뒤집어서 양쪽 다 익힐까?
B: 그냥 양쪽 다 익혀.

대화 37

A: I'm here to see a doctor. I'm not feeling well.
B: Can you please tell me your symptoms?
A: 진찰을 받으러 왔어요. 몸이 안 좋아요.
B: 증상을 말씀해 주시겠어요?

A: I have a fever and my head hurts.
B: How long have you been sick?
A: 열이 나고 머리가 아파요.
B: 얼마 동안 아팠어요?

A: Did all of your family come home on your birthday?
B: Yes, except my sister. She couldn't come home because of her job.
A: 가족들 모두 네 생일에 집에 왔니?
B: 응, 우리 언니만 빼고. 언니는 일 때문에 못 왔어.

대화 38

A: There are many opportunities here at this company.
B: Chances are we will get promoted too if we work hard.
A: 이 회사에는 기회가 아주 많아요.
B: 우리도 열심히 일하면 승진할 수 있어요.

A: You wanna get a drink after work?
B: No, I'm going to be working late.
A: Still working on that big project?
B: Yeah. Will you help me?
A: 퇴근하고 한 잔 하면 좋겠니?
B: 아니, 나 야근할 거야.
A: 아직도 그 대형 프로젝트 하고 있어?
B: 응. 도와줄래?

A: I'm gonna help you out with this project.
B: I've got enough help.
A: It will take some of the load off of you.
A: 내가 이 프로젝트를 도와줄게.
B: 난 충분히 도움을 받았어.
A: 네 짐을 덜어줄 거라고.

대화 39

A: That sweater looks really expensive.

B: It cost a lot of money.

A: Well, it looks really good on you.

A: 그 스웨터 정말 비싸 보인다.

B: 돈을 좀 많이 들였지.

A: 음, 정말 너한테 잘 어울린다.

A: Whatever happens, I try to look on the bright side.

B: That's what I like the most about you.

A: 무슨 일이 있어도, 난 좋은 쪽으로 생각하려고 노력해.

B: 그게 너에 대해 제일 마음에 드는 점이야.

A: When is the best time for us to go hiking tomorrow?

B: How does 6 AM sound?

A: That's rather early. How about 7 AM instead of 6?

A: 우리, 내일 언제 등산하러 가면 제일 좋을까요?

B: 아침 6시 어때요?

A: 그건 좀 이른데요. 6시 말고 7시 어때요?

대화 40

A: Where do you wanna vacation this summer?
B: I don't care. You wanna pick?
A: Well, you wanna head to the beach?
B: Actually, I'd love to go to the mountain again.
A: 올 여름에 휴가를 어디로 가고 싶니?
B: 상관없어. 네가 고를래?
A: 음, 해변으로 가고 싶니?
B: 사실 난 산으로 다시 가면 좋겠어.

A: Where should we hold the awards dinner?
B: We should check the budget first.
A: 시상식 만찬을 어디에서 열어야 할까요?
B: 예산부터 확인해야겠어요.

A: You can't wear that into the meeting.
B: I don't have anything nicer to wear.
A: You gotta go shopping.
A: 회의에 그런 옷을 입고 갈 순 없어.
B: 난 입을 만한 괜찮은 옷이 없어.
A: 넌 쇼핑해야겠다.

대화 41

A: Could you tell me how to get to Dallas from here?
B: It's a half hour drive from here. I'll draw a map showing the way to Dallas from here.
A: 여기서 댈러스로 어떻게 가는지 알려주시겠어요?
B: 여기서 차로 30분 걸려요. 여기서 댈러스까지 가는 길을 약도로 그려드릴게요.

A: Oh, there's a good dog park around here.
B: Shall we drive there with our dog today?
A: 아, 근처에 애견 공원 좋은 게 있네.
B: 우리 오늘 우리 강아지 데리고 거기 가볼까?

A: I have nothing to give to you this holiday.
B: Are you telling me that you're completely broke?
A: 이번 명절에 너한테 줄 게 없네.
B: 지금 너, 완전히 빈털터리라는 거니?

대화 42

A: How did you decide on your career?
B: Well, I've never thought about my career seriously.
A: 네 진로를 어떻게 결정했어?
B: 음, 난 내가 할 일에 대해서 그렇게 진지하게 생각해본 적이 없어.

A: I'm interested in booking flight tickets for myself from Boston to New York City.
B: I can help you with that. Would you like to book return fare, and are there any preferred travel dates?
A: 보스턴에서 뉴욕까지 가는 비행기 표를 예약하고 싶어요.
B: 왕복 요금으로 예약하시겠어요, 그리고 원하는 날짜가 있으신지요?

A: We're running out of gas.
B: I know. Let's drop by the gas station.
A: Don't top off the gas tank. It can spill.
A: 우리 기름이 다 떨어져 가는데.
B: 그러네. 주유소에 좀 들르자.
A: 기름을 가득 채우지 마. 기름이 새어 나올 수 있어요.

대화 43

A: Last thing I want to do is work all weekend.
B: Did you have plans this weekend?
A: I need to go shopping for a new coat.
A: 난 절대 주말 내내 일하는 건 하고 싶지 않아.
B: 이번 주말에 계획 있어?
A: 새 코트를 사러 쇼핑 가야 해.

A: I don't know how much I can help. Sam might be a better choice to help you.
B: I don't know who Sam is.
B: He works in the office.
A: 내가 얼마나 도움이 될지 모르겠어. 샘이 너를 더 잘 도와줄 거야.
B: 샘이 누군지 몰라.
B: 그는 사무실에서 일해.

A: Did you see my new hiking gear?
B: Yes. Where did you get it? Wow, you really lucked out.
A: 내가 새로 산 등산용품 봤어?
B: 응. 어디서 산 거야? 와, 진짜 운이 좋았네.

대화 44

A: Have you ever gone waterskiing?
B: No, I can't say I have.
A: I hear it's great fun!
A: 수상스키 타러 가본 적 있니?
B: 아니, 가본 적 없는 것 같은데.
A: 정말 재미있더라!

A: Why do you want to go to the cafe at night?
B: I want to see my friends.
A: Do you want me to go with?
B: I wish you would.
A: 왜 밤에 카페에 가려고 하니?
B: 친구들을 만나려고.
A: 내가 같이 가줄까?
B: 그래 줬으면 좋겠어.

대화 45

A: I need to book a flight to LA.
B: Ok, is this a one-way or round trip ticket?
A: LA로 가는 항공권을 예약하고 싶습니다.
B: 네, 편도입니까, 왕복입니까?

A: When was the last time you went to the movies?
B: I can't remember. It's been a while.
A: You really need to take a break from your studies.
A: 너 영화 보러 마지막으로 간 게 언제야?
B: 기억이 안 나. 꽤 됐지.
A: 넌 정말 공부만 하지 말고 좀 쉴 필요가 있어.

A: My TV is broken. I'm sick of having to fix things myself.
B: Broken? That's a bummer.
A: 내 TV가 고장 났어. 나는 뭔가를 내가 고쳐야 하는 게 지겨워.
B: 고장 났다고? 그거 안됐네.

대화 46

A: What do you usually do after work?
B: I like taking a walk in the evening.
A: Do you have a favorite place you like to go to?
B: Yeah, I like walking under the bridge at the park.
A: Myself, I prefer to walk on the street.
B: That's also a favorite place of mine.
A: 퇴근 후에 주로 뭐하니?
B: 나는 저녁에 산책하는 걸 좋아해.
A: 좋아하는 장소가 있니?
B: 응, 난 공원에서 다리 아래를 걷는 걸 좋아해.
A: 난 거리를 걷는 걸 더 좋아하는데.
B: 거기도 내가 좋아하는 장소야.

A: Would you have any reason to be late?
B: I didn't have any clothes to wear.
A: All you have to do is change your shirt.
A: 늦을 만한 이유가 있니?
B: 입을 옷이 없었어.
A: 넌 셔츠만 갈아 입으면 돼.

대화 47

A: Sorry, I didn't mean to cut in front of you.
B: It's no problem. You seem to be busy. I'm in no rush at all.
A: You are very understanding.
A: 죄송해요. 앞에 끼어들려는 건 아니었어요.
B: 괜찮아요. 바쁘신 것 같네요. 저 하나도 안 바빠요.
A: 이해심이 많으시네요.

A: I'm worried about how much you've been working.
B: I'm doing okay.
A: You seem really tired.
B: I feel fine.
A: 네가 일을 너무 많이 하는 것 같아서 걱정이 돼.
B: 괜찮아.
A: 너 정말 피곤해 보여.
A: 난 괜찮아.

대화 48

A: Is it true that it always rains in the UK?
B: Well, not exactly, but maybe there's a little bit of truth in that.
A: 영국에서는 항상 비가 내린다는 게 사실인가요?
B: 글쎄요, 꼭 그런 건 아니지만, 어느 정도는 사실이에요.

A: Is unemployment a big problem in Korea?
B: Well, it is an issue, but it's not as bad as a few years ago.
A: 한국에서 실업이 큰 문제인가요?
B: 음, 문제이긴 한데요, 몇 년 전만큼 나쁘진 않아요.

A: Do you happen to know when the meeting starts?
B: It's at 3:00 in my office.
A: Will you tell me where your office is?
A: 혹시 몇 시에 회의 시작하는지 알고 있나요?
B: 3시에 제 사무실에서 할 거예요.
A: 당신 사무실이 어디에요?

대화 49

A: Is this your first visit here?
B: No, I've been here before on business. It's a great city.
A: 여기 처음 방문이세요?
B: 아니요, 출장으로 전에 와 봤어요. 멋진 도시죠.

A: Do you do any sport in your free time?
B: Yes, I go to the gym and I do a bit of jogging, but only to keep fit.
A: 시간 날 때 운동하세요?
B: 네, 체육관에 가서 조깅을 하는데 몸매를 유하려고 하는 거예요.

A: Did you have a nice dinner yesterday?
B: Yes, we did. My husbund cooked up a salmon for the main course.
A: 어제 저녁은 맛있게 먹었니?
B: 응, 남편이 주 요리로 연어 요리를 만들어 줬어.

대화 50

A: I'm going there by subway. Which station is the most convenient to get there?
B: Which lane do you take?
A: 제가 지금 지하철을 타고서 가는 중인데요. 어느 역에서 내리는 것이 가기가 편한가요?
B: 몇 호선을 타고 계십니까?

A: How is Busan? Is everything okay?
B: Yes. I have a meeting this afternoon with Mr. Kim from ABC.
A: 부산은 어때요? 모두 잘 진행되고 있나요?
B: 네. 오후에 ABC 사의 김 고장과 회의가 있어요.

A: You might want to bring an umbrella today.
B: Why do you say that? Is it supposed to rain?
A: 오늘 우산 가져가는 게 좋겠어.
B: 왜? 오늘 비가 온대?

대화 51

A: What did you think of the report?
B: You don't need to change anything. You just need to present it to the teacher.
A: I'm really nervous.
B: I'm sure you'll do great!
A: Last think I want to do is present the report.
B: You did a great job on it!
A: 보고서에 대해 어떻게 생각해?
B: 넌 아무 것도 바꿀 필요가 없어. 선생님께 제출하기만 하면 돼.
A: 정말 긴장이 돼.
B: 넌 잘 할 거라고 믿어.
A: 난 정말 보고서 제출을 하고 싶지 않아.
B: 보고서 정말 잘 썼어!

A: Can I go to work with you for a couple of hours?
B: Weren't you planning to have a job interview?
A: I was, but I didn't know it's been rescheduled.
A: 몇 시간 동안만 너랑 같이 회사가도 될까?
B: 너 면접 보기로 하지 않았니?
A: 그랬는데, 시간이 바뀐 지 몰랐어.

대화 52

A: Will you keep an eye on my dog for me?
B: Sure. Where are you going?
A: I'm heading to the coast for the weekend.
B: I'm totally jealous. Can I join you?
A: 우리 개 좀 봐줄래?
B: 그럴게. 어디 가는데?
A: 주말에 바닷가에 가려고.
B: 정말 좋겠다. 나도 같이 가면 안 될까?

A: How would you like your hair cut?
B: Cut it short, please.
A: 머리를 어떻게 잘라드릴까요?
B: 짧게 잘라주세요.

A: Do you prefer a hotel downtown or near the airport?
B: I prefer a hotel downtown.
A: 시내 호텔이 좋으세요, 공항 근처 호텔이 좋으세요?
B: 시내 호텔이 더 좋아요.

대화 53

A: Would you like to talk about this?
B: What is there to talk about?
A: Let's take some time off.
B. I told you I can't.
A: 이것에 대해 얘기를 하고 싶니?
B: 얘기할 게 뭐가 있어?
A: 며칠 쉬자.
B: 난 그럴 수 없다고 말했잖아.

A: What do your family plan to do on Christmas morning?
B: We're going to have breakfast and then open our presents.
A: 크리스마스 아침에 너희 가족들은 뭘 할 거니?
B: 아침을 먹고 난 뒤 선물을 풀어볼 거야.

대화 54

A: It's hard to leave work at a reasonable hour.
B: Yes. I rarely have time to see my kids these days.
A: 제 시간에 퇴근하기가 어렵네요.
B: 네. 전 요즘 애들하고 보낼 시간이 거의 없어요.

A: You look pale and sweaty.
B: You're right. I have a cold. Don't come near me.
A: I could tell by looking that he was sick.
A: 너 창백하고 식은땀을 흘리는 것 같구나.
B: 맞아. 감기 걸렸어. 나한테 가까이 오지 마.
A: 보니까 그가 아프다는 것을 알겠더라고.

A: You look fatter today. I think you gotta start working out.
B: I know, I'm trying.
A: I'll help you.
A: 너 오늘은 더 살쪄 보여. 넌 운동 시작해야 할 것 같아.
B: 알아. 노력하고 있어.
A: 도와줄게.

대화 55

A: Which season of the year do you like the best?
B: I love the summer weather.
A: What's the weather like during summer in Korea?
B: It's usually hot, wet, and humid.
A: But, why do you like summer?
B: I can enjoy the summer spots.
A: 어느 계절을 제일 좋아해요?
B: 여름이요.
A: 한국의 여름 날씨는 어때요?
B: 보통 무덥고 비도 많이 오고 후덥지근하죠.
A: 그런데 왜 여름을 좋아하죠?
B: 여름 스포츠를 즐길 수 있으니까요.

A: You gotta eat better.
B: What do you mean?
A: You're gaining a lot of weight.
A: 넌 좀 잘 먹어야만 해.
B: 무슨 말이야?
A: 너 살이 많이 찌고 있어.

대화 56

A: No! I overslept again. I turned the alarm off in my sleep.
B: You're gonna be late for your class.
A: I'm sure the professor won't understand.
A: 이런! 내가 또 늦잠을 잤어. 알람을 잠결에 꺼버렸나 봐.
B: 넌 수업에 늦겠다.
A: 교수님은 절대 이해해주시지 않을 거예요.

A: Karaoke was fun yesterday. You sing very well.
B: Oh, I enjoy singing.
A: 어제 가라오케가 재미있더군요. 노래 잘 하시네요.
B: 아, 전 노래 부르는 걸 좋아해요.

A: I gotta break up with him. He cheated on me.
B: Are you kidding me? But you really liked him.
A: 난 그 사람하고 헤어져야만 해. 그가 나 몰래 바람 피웠어.
B: 농담하는 거지? 하지만 넌 정말 그를 좋아했잖아.

대화 57

A: I slept through the staff meeting.
B: Don't worry.
A: Our boss is not very forgiving.
B: You can always think up a good excuse.
A: 직원 회의를 하다가 자 버렸어.
B: 걱정하지 마.
A: 우리 상사는 그다지 너그러운 분이 아니신데.
B: 늘 그럴싸한 핑계를 꾸며내면 되지.

A: You're telling me you're leaving?
B: Yes, I found a job in Seoul.
A: 그래서 네가 지금 떠난다고 말하고 있는 거야?
B: 그래, 서울에서 일자리를 구했거든.

A: You turned the wrong way.
B: What?
A: I was just saying that we are lost.
A: 길을 잘못 들었어.
B: 뭐라고?
A: 난 우리가 길을 잃었다고 했을 뿐이야.

대화 58

A: Damn, I have to work overtime again.
B: I'll get home after midnight again.
A: 젠장, 나 또 야근해야 해.
B: 또 자정 넘어 들어가겠군.

A: These hiccups are killing me. They won't stop.
B: Drink a glass of water quickly.
A: It's not helpful.
B: Hold your breath as long as you can.
A: 이 딸꾹질 때문에 죽겠네. 멈추지를 않아.
B: 물 한 잔을 빨리 마셔봐.
A: 도움이 안 돼.
B: 참을 수 있을 만큼 숨을 참아봐.

대화 59

A: We still need a few things from the market.
B: I was gonna go tomorrow. Do we need a lot of things?
A: All we need is milk.
A: 아직 마켓에서 몇 가지 살 게 있어.
B: 내일 가려고 했어. 필요한 게 많아?
A: 우유만 있으면 돼.

A: I wonder when this wet weather will clear up?
B: I'm sick and tired of this hot, muggy weather.
A: It seems that we're in the middle of the monsoon season.
A: 언제쯤 비가 그치려나?
B: 덥고 눅눅한 것도 이젠 지겹다 지겨워.
A: 지금이 우기인 것 같아.

대화 60

A: Having to deal with my boss all day is so stressful.
B: He never stops talking once he opens his mouth.
A: 우리 상사 같은 사람을 종일 대하자니 스트레스 쌓여.
B: 그는 한번 입을 열면 말을 멈추지 않아.

A: We have to plan our company outing. When do you have time?
B: I'm available for lunch anytime.
A: 회사 야유회 계획을 세워야 해요. 언제 시간이 나세요?
B: 점심식사 때는 언제든 시간이 됩니다.

A: My boss let me know I was fired.
B: Don't tell me another lie.
A: 내 상사가 내게 내가 해고당했다고 알려줬지.
B: 설마 또 거짓말은 아니겠죠.

랜덤 테스트

우리말 영어로 말해보기

A: _____

B: Me neither. Some snack this morning is all I've eaten today.

A: 전 아침 10시 이후로 아무것도 못 먹었어요.
B: 저도요. 오늘 아침에 간식 먹은 게 다예요.

A: _____ in Korea apart from football?

B: Well, lots of people are into baseball and _____,
too.

A: 축구를 제외하고 한국에서 가장 큰 스포츠가 뭐에요?
B: 음, 많은 사람들이 야구에 빠져 있고 농구도 매우 인기 있어요.

A: What is this?

_____

B: Of course, because it's tuna kimchi soup.

A: I don't like it.

A: 이게 뭐야? 비린내가 나.
B: 당연하지. 참치 김치찌개니까 그렇지.
A: 난 그걸 좋아하지 않아.

A: _____

B: Why not?

A: I don't know, but I can't stop thinking about her. She's super smart and pretty attractive.

A: 아직 그녀한테 데이트 신청도 안 했어.

B: 왜 안했어?

A: 나도 모르겠어. 하지만 그녀 생각을 멈출 수가 없어. 그녀는 무지하게 똑똑하고 매력적이야.

A: You need to talk to Jinsu.

B: _____

A: We're gonna see him later.

B: _____

A: 넌 진수와 얘기 좀 해야 해.
B: 걘 절대로 전화를 받으려 하지 않을 거야.
A: 우린 나중에 그를 만나게 될 거야.
B: 오늘 저녁에 걔한테 말해볼게.

A: We've got a lot to do.

B: _____

A: 우린 아직 할 일이 많아요.
B: 이 초과근무 때문에 짜증나요.

A: _____

B: I know. It took me an hour just to shovel the driveway before I left today.

A: 눈이 그칠 것 같지 않네요!
B: 그러니까요. 오늘 출발하기 전에 진입로까지 삽질을 하느라 한 시간이나 걸렸어요.

A: I could eat ramyon every meal of the day.

B: _____

A: 나는 끼니마다 다 라면을 먹을 수도 있어.
B: 그건 그렇게 건강에 좋을 것 같지 않아.

A: I decided to _____

_____

B: Sounds really motivating

.

A: 나는 공공 도서관에서 하루 종일 시간
을 보내기로 했어.
B: 정말 의욕적인 것 같네.

A: We really need to get out more.

B: So, _____

A: 우린 좀 더 자주 나가서 놀아야 할 것
같아.
B: 그럼, 나랑 영화 보러 갈래?

A: _____

B: Yes, let's stop off at the bar across the bank.

A: 진짜 한잔 하고 싶은데.
B: 그래. 은행 길건너에 있는 바에 들르자.

A: I'm planning on taking the family to England.

B: Yes, in fact I went last summer.

A: 영국으로 가족을 데리고 가려고요. 가
본 적 있어요?
B: 네, 사실 지난 여름에 갔었어요.

A: What about the dinner?

_____

B: I love Korean cuisine. Thanks for your treat.

A: 저녁 식사는 어떠셨나요? 음식이 괜찮았나요?
B: 전 한국 음식을 좋아해요. 대접해 주셔서 고마워요.

A: I love it when the week winds down.

B: Yes, _____

A: 나는 한 주가 끝나가는 주말이 참 좋아.

B: 그래, 우리 가족들이랑 시간을 더 많이 보낼 수가 있잖아.

A: Are you in a hurry?

B: Yes, my friend _____

_____

A: 바쁘세요?
B: 네, 친구가 차에서 기다리고 있어요.

A: My son slept late this morning, so I

_____

B: Oh, it's already 8 o'clock. Hurry up, but drive safely.

A: 아들이 아침에 늦잠을 자서 아들을 학교에 내려 줘야 해요.
B: 어머, 벌써 8시에요. 서둘러요, 하지만 조심히 운전하고요.

A: Look at this picture. I want to take those trains sometime.

B: Then _____

A: Sounds nice. Let's decide when to go.

A: 이 사진 좀 봐. 언젠가는 그 기차들을 타보고 싶어.
B: 그럼 우리 이번 달에 한번 타보는 게 어때?
A: 좋아. 우리 언제 갈지 결정하자.

A: I think _____

_____

B: That's a great idea. How about this one?

A: 이 상품 사진을 저희 광고에도 사용할 수 있을 것 같은데요.
B: 좋은 생각이에요. 이건 어때요?

A: Where are you going?

B: I'm gonna go to the movies.

A: _____
There's gonna be a long line.

A: 뭐 할 거니?
B: 영화 보러 가게 될 거야.
A: 지금 가는 게 좋을 거야. 줄이 길 거
거든.

A: _____ to the symphony with me?

B: When would you like to go?

A: 저랑 음악회에 갈 시간 있으세요?
B: 언제 가고 싶으신데요?

A: What is that?   .

_____

A: We should get the recipe.

A: 그거 뭐야? 닭고기 맛이 나.
B: 만드는 법을 알아가야 겠다.

A: _____

How tall are you?

B: One meter 87 centimeters.

A: 당신은 보통 사람보다 키가 좀 크군
요. 키가 얼마나 되요?
B: 1미터 87센티미터에요.

A: I'd like to take a shuttle bus.

_____

B: You may stand in line here.

A: 셔틀버스를 타려고 하는데요. 티켓은
어디서 사나요?
B: 여기 줄을 서면 됩니다.

A: I sleep through the alarm very often.

B: _____

A: 난 자주 알람소리를 못 듣고 자.
B: 스마트폰 알람을 세 번 맞춰 놓아봐.

A: How do you like the atmosphere at this place?

B: _____

A: Then, we can stay a little longer.

A: 여기 분위기 어때?
B: 팔팔한데.
A: 그러면 좀 더 있자.

A: How long does it take to get to Wall
Street?

B: _____

A: 월스트리트까지 얼마나 걸리나요?
B: 교통 상황에 달려 있어요.

A: I'll see you tomorrow at the zoo!

_____

B: I'm sure the weather will be fine.

_____

A: 내일 동물원에서 보자!
비가 안 왔으면 좋겠다.
B: 날씨는 좋을 거야. 점심 싸오는 거 잊
지 마.

A: _____

B: A small car with good gas mileage, if possible.

A: 어떤 종류를 렌트하려고 하시죠?
B: 되도록 연비가 좋은 소형차요.

A: We're going to eat dinner together tonight.

B: Since I don't drink,

_____

A: 오늘 다 같이 저녁 회식을 할 거에요.
B: 전 술을 마시지 않으니 제가 운전해 드릴게요.

A: _____

B: I don't think we'll be late. I'll drive a little faster.

A: 우리 늦지 않았으면 좋겠다.
B: 늦지 않을 거야. 좀 더 빨리 운전할게.